CURES WORSE THAN THE DISEASE

Mom, Suddenly I'm Feeling Much Better

Lots of times when you have a cold or the flu, your parents give you cough syrup so you'll feel better. Sometimes it's hard to swallow cough syrup. It tastes bitter and the strong flavor makes you gag. But think about this the next time your parents pull out a bottle and a spoon: in 1865, people thought that a soup made from 50 frogs would cure a cough!

Smile. I Want To See Your War Trophies

The defeat of the French Emperor Napoleon Bonaparte at the Battle of Waterloo in 1815 was a bonanza for European dentists. Shrewd local residents yanked the teeth from the mouths of the dead soldiers and sold them by the pound to manufacturers. They, in turn, fashioned the stolen choppers into sets of false teeth. Known as "Waterloo Teeth," these dentures made from the strong, healthy teeth of the young men who fought the battle were much sought after by toothless older people.

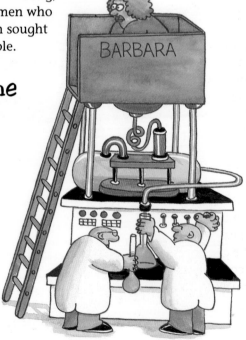

I'll Just Try Some Warm Milk

In Germany during the 1860s, drug researchers developed drugs to help patients who had trouble relaxing or sleeping. This group of drugs was made from human urine donated by a woman named Barbara — which is why these drugs are called "barbiturates."

GROSS FACTS TO BLOW YOUR MIND

Illustrated by Skip Morrow

Written by Judith Freeman Clark & Stephen Long

A New England Publishing Associates Book

PRICE STERN SLOAN
Los Angeles

A New England Publishing Associates Book

Published by Price Stern Sloan, Inc.
11150 Olympic Boulevard, Los Angeles, California 90064

ISBN: 0-8431-3578-6

Library of Congress Catalog Number: 93-12250

Library of Congress Cataloging-in-Publication Data

Clark, Judith Freeman.
    Gross Facts to blow your mind by Judith Freeman Clark;
illustrated by Skip Morrow.
        p.   cm. — (Facts to blow your mind)
    Summary: Presents "bizarre" information, such as spitting laws and
customs.
    ISBN 0-8431-3578-6 : $4.99
    1. Curiosities and wonders — Juvenile literature.   (1. Curiosities
and wonders.) I. Morrow, Skip, Ill. II. Title. III. Series:
Clark, Judith Freemen, Facts to blow your mind.
AG243.C5637   1993
031.02 — dc20   93-12250
                                                         CIP
                                                         AC

Table of Contents

Here's Something To Chase That Nagging Headache Away

If you've ever stepped on skunk cabbage, you know how this plant got its name. Despite, or perhaps because of, its foul smell, the Micmac Indians of New England once used this plant to cure headaches. Sufferers were advised to pick some skunk cabbage, squish the leaves together, and inhale deeply. Apparently, the horrible odor quickly made you forget any throbbing or other sensations in your head.

Doc, Are You Sure This Doesn't Have Any Side Effects?

During the Black Plague of the 14th century, many doctors tried to come up with a cure for the dread illness, which was almost always fatal. A few remedies included rubbing the body with — and drinking — goat urine, standing in front of a latrine and inhaling deeply, putting dried toads on plague boils, and rubbing the guts of a newborn dog on the sick person's forehead.

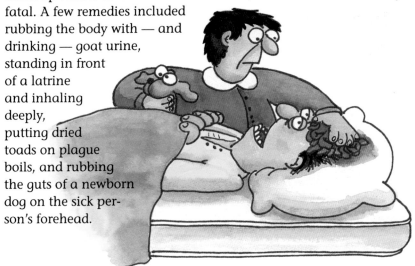

A Dead Bat A Day Keeps The Doctor Away

When your mother tells you to put on an extra sweater before going outside to play, she's doing it because she wants you to stay healthy. She might also insist that you take vitamins or carry an umbrella when it rains. In the Middle Ages, mothers believed their kids wouldn't get sick if they hung bags containing pieces of dead bats from their necks.

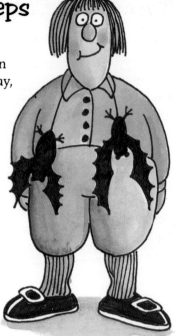

Preventive Medicine

Today, some people believe drinking orange juice or eating lots of chicken soup can ward off the flu or a cold. Maybe they're right. Centuries ago, people were equally convinced that they could avoid the evil spirits that brought on sickness if they rubbed themselves with a lotion of bear fat, dog fat, "rain worm" oil and spider oil!

Take Some Camel Dung And Call Me In The Morning

In the Sahara Desert, where camels are among the few domesticated animals, people have found lots of uses for camel dung. When it's dry, people burn it and cook dinner over the fire. But when it's still fresh and moist, people stuff it in their noses to help cure head colds.

Let's Get Pickled

In Elizabethan England, people who got sick with smallpox were stuck in a vat normally used for pickling meat. In the vat, they were fumigated with a red powder called cinnabar and then forced to sweat profusely. Afterward, they were given only enough food to keep them from starving. Not surprisingly, some people didn't get better.

This Tooth Bugs Me

In ancient Europe, people were convinced that crushed ladybugs had the power to stop toothaches. A person could place the dead bug on the problem tooth, and the pain would instantly disappear.

Available At Better Pharmacies

In the 16th century, something called mummy balm was a popular "cure" for several diseases, including gout and the common cold. It's doubtful that this medicine really worked, though, since the chief ingredient was powdered Egyptian mummies.

DIRTY WORK

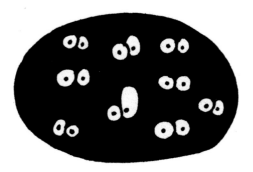

I Only Have Eyes For You

Bird droppings, or guano, can be useful to scientists studying what birds eat. For example, scientists discovered that some penguins eat krill — microscopic sea animals — by pawing through piles of bird poop and discovering dozens of undigested krill eyes staring up at them through the guano.

Honest, Officer, I Was Just Doing My Homework

Medical students today cut open dead bodies to study how they work. During the Middle Ages, it was illegal to dissect human corpses except those of criminals burned at the stake. Since there weren't enough of these to go around, students often were caught in graveyards, stealing dead bodies of law-abiding citizens for their medical studies.

Nosy Researchers

Scientists at a U.S. university are studying rhinotillexomania, a fancy word for nose picking. Some questions they're asking people are, "Which finger do you use?" and, "Do you look at what you pull out?"

Care For Some Pepper?

Small, gray and shaped like a fat worm, the common slug is a real garden pest. Experienced gardeners know there's a speedy way to kill the slimy creatures. Just sprinkle them with salt: as the sodium hits the slug, its soft body swells up like a balloon and literally explodes. Then the slug carcass shrivels into a small spot of yellowish slime.

This Job Isn't For Everyone

If you've studied ancient Egypt, you probably know the Egyptians came up with a special process called embalming to preserve the human body as a "mummy" after death. The process was a sacred part of the Egyptian reli-

gion, but you have to wonder how much Egyptian embalmers were paid. It required about eight months to transform a dead body into a mummy. During the process, the embalmer removed all of the dead person's internal organs, including the brain, which was pulled out with long brass hooks through the nostrils!

The Big Bang Theory

One of the ingredients in gunpowder is saltpeter, which develops naturally on the damp, manure-covered walls of stables. There were so many wars in Europe during the 1700s and 1800s that armies ran short of saltpeter produced this old-fashioned way. Eventually, the government ordered citizens to build "nitre" beds to increase supplies. To do this, they piled up garbage, cow, sheep and even human manure, covered it with a roof and then doused it periodically with blood from slaughterhouses. In France, the Emperor Napoleon Bonaparte even ordered his people to urinate on the nitre beds to stimulate production of the saltpeter he needed to make war on the rest of Europe.

Skin And Bones

Animal skeletons in museum exhibits are clean, without a speck of flesh on them. Obviously someone — or something — has to work carefully to remove the animal's flesh to prepare the skeletons for display. At Yale University's Natural History Museum, scientists keep carrion beetles on hand in a special "bug room" for this purpose. The insects strip away the meat from the bones of animal skeletons, usually in just a few hours! The scientists then wash the remaining bones in ammonia (to remove any leftover meat or beetles) before putting the skeletons on exhibit.

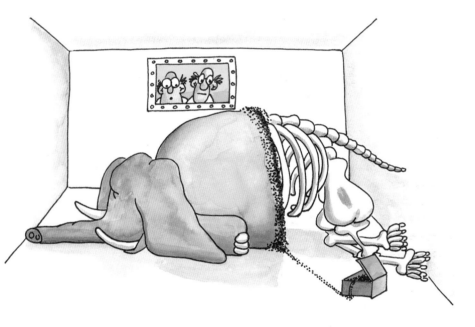

Food & Drink:
Plain, Fancy & Wholesome

Go Pick Your Own Maggots!

When the Native Americans in the wild and remote northern parts of Alberta, Canada want a snack, they can't run down to a convenience store and buy a bag of candy. Instead, they just find the nearest caribou, the reindeer-like animals they raise. Certain flies lay their eggs on the caribou hide, and the eggs hatch into maggots. Local kids stroll through the herd, pick the wiggly creatures off, then pop them into their mouths for a quick and tasty snack.

Care For Some Ground Glass On Your Salad?

We like to be sure the food we eat is good for us. This is one reason restaurants must be licensed and government agencies check to make sure food is pure and healthy. Before laws protecting food purity were passed in the early 20th century, manufacturers secretly added all sorts of junk to food. They put sawdust in flour, plaster in milk, and sand in sugar. Rats and bugs fell into sausage-making machines. Other disgusting ingredients were added, too. One offender was caught filling jars of grated cheese with pulverized umbrella handles!

Here Kitty, Time For Dinner!

In France today, some people consider horse meat quite a delicacy. A few centuries ago, many people thought eating horse meat was gross. It just seemed wrong to wolf down chunks of an animal that served people so faithfully in so many ways. These more sensitive souls often preferred to eat less useful creatures— like cats and dogs!

You Look Good Enough To Eat

To prehistoric people, bone marrow was a delicious snack. Scientists have uncovered sites where bones have been cracked open, sucked dry, and tossed aside. Our Stone Age ancestors were not very fussy about what they ate either. Some of the chewed-up bones were from sheep, boar, deer — and humans.

Cheers!

More than a thousand lizards are killed to make a single bottle of Chinese Red Spotted Lizard Wine.

Just What The Doctor Ordered

Butter is delicious on hot toast or a stack of pancakes, but many doctors suggest using margarine instead. The doctors say butter and other dairy products increase a fatty substance in your blood called cholesterol, which is bad for your heart. Margarine may be good for you, but you wouldn't think so from reading the list of ingredients. The typical margarine recipe includes pig fat, beef fat, and herring fat. Yellow dye is added to cover up its real color: gray.

What Goes Around, Comes Around

The Boston Cooking-School Cookbook has a half-dozen or so recipes for honey-comb tripe. You can broil it, bake it, or fry it in butter. People who eat it say tripe is a real delicacy. Do you know what tripe is? It's the stomach lining of a cow or an ox.

Hunger Is The Best Sauce

Even cannibals have their favorite recipes. One involves burying the victim's body for about a week, then digging it up. The cook scrapes all the maggots off the body and onto banana leaves. The meat and bones are chopped up and cooked together in an oven, then served separately from the maggots, which are considered delicious.

A Thirst-Quenching Drink

Aztec priests in Mexico during the 1500s had elaborate methods of human sacrifice. In one of the more gruesome Aztec rituals, a human heart was cut, still beating, from a living man. As the blood gushed from the severed aorta, the priest put a straw into the opening and sucked up the victim's blood.

From Head To Toe

The next time your mother goes shopping and asks if you want something from the store, why don't you ask her to pick up some head cheese? Head cheese is a jellied loaf or sausage made from the head, feet, heart and tongue of a pig.

Can I Have A Tuna Sandwich?

Hot dogs are a favorite lunch food in almost every school cafeteria. This isn't surprising because sausages and hot dogs have been around for more than 3,000 years. Have you ever thought about what goes into a hot dog? Animal intestines were generally used as the casing — or skin — for early hot dogs, and many brands still use these natural casings today. Some pretty unpleasant- sounding things are stuffed inside — just look at the package label the next time your parents buy hot dogs. If you put on enough mustard and relish, you won't be able to taste those beef lips and pigs' tongues.

Mom, Could I Have A Pizza Instead?

Beef stew probably won't make most kids' list of ten favorite foods. If that's what's for dinner tonight, you can probably swallow it. If you had been a kid during medieval times, 600 to 800 years ago, the equally boring but ever- popular dinner with parents was hedgehog stew.

Good And Crunchy

Most of us love to dig into a big bag of potato chips. In the past and in some parts of the world, people have enjoyed eating things that would make us gag. At feasts in ancient Rome, a popular dish was flamingo tongues. In some parts of South Africa, people roast termites and eat them by the handful—just like we eat potato chips!

Just Some Water, Please

The native people of Central America are fond of a drink called "chicha." Made from bananas or pineapples, it is prepared by young girls who chew the fruit thoroughly before spitting it out. The gob is then allowed to ferment into the favorite local beverage.

Sweet Tooth

If you go shopping for candy at an island market in the West Indies, watch out! You may ask for a chocolate bar but instead get a special honey-like candy popular among the people of the islands. Some of this candy, while delicious, is made from a mixture of white ants and banana flour!

Thanks, I'll Just Have A Green Salad

It's pretty easy to get "fresh meat" these days. We just go to the supermarket, pick out a steak, chop, or roast and pay for it. That "fresh" red meat sold isn't really as fresh as we like to think. In fact, it's more than 10 days old! If the butcher put meat out for sale any earlier, it would still show signs of rigor mortis — that's the muscle stiffness that occurs when an animal is slaughtered. So the meat we buy isn't fresh at all. It's really in an early stage of decay!

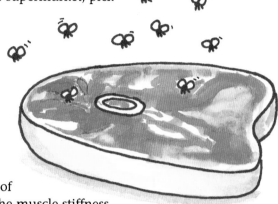

Is It Time For A Break?

Like workers everywhere, those in Japanese silk factories enjoy breaking for a snack during their workdays. Their snacks are just a little unusual. During the manufacture of silk, each cocoon is unwound to produce a thread of silk. This process also reveals the silkworm grub, which is no longer useful — at least in the making of silk thread. The silk workers say the grub worm, when fried, is quite tasty.

SECRETS OF GOOD GROOMING

There's No Grimy Bathtub Ring In The Palace ...

Today, our homes have sinks, showers and bathtubs. Our parents constantly remind us to wash our faces, shampoo our hair, or shower after playing outside. Adults haven't always worried so much about dirt! In fact, up to a few hundred years ago many people thought too much washing was vain and unhealthy. Queen Elizabeth I of England was considered a cleanliness fanatic because she took one bath a month—whether she needed it or not!

This Sounds A Little Bit Fishy

The U.S. Government has strict rules about what ingredients can be used in cosmetics. This is because 70 to 100 years ago poisonous materials were used in women's makeup, and many women became sick from using them. Even today some pretty strange things are mixed together to make cosmetics. One of the most common is fish scales soaked in ammonia — often used in lipsticks and eye shadows! Beeswax is used in all kinds of makeup. Beeswax comes from vomit thrown up by female worker bees.

Only Their Hairdressers Know For Sure

Men and women in ancient Rome who wanted to lighten their hair only had to go as far as the nearest park. That's where they could pick up a favorite Roman hair bleach: pigeon poop.

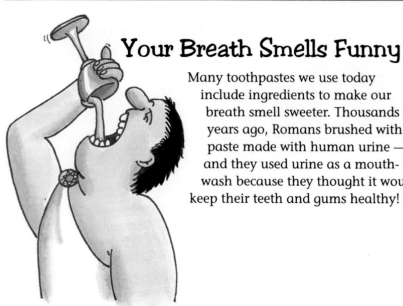

Your Breath Smells Funny

Many toothpastes we use today include ingredients to make our breath smell sweeter. Thousands of years ago, Romans brushed with a paste made with human urine — and they used urine as a mouthwash because they thought it would keep their teeth and gums healthy!

Get Out Your Handkerchief

If you sneeze a lot when you have a cold, you can probably sympathize with sheep who are attacked by nose bots. These are flies that plant their eggs on the edge of a sheep's nostril. The eggs hatch into grubs that work their way up the nostril into the sheep's sinuses. By now about an inch long, the grubs crawl around and make it difficult for the sheep to breathe. This causes them to sneeze. Next time you sneeze, be thankful you're not a sheep.

Why Are You Scratching Your Head?

Sometimes kids get sent home because their teacher discovers they have head lice. For a lot of kids (and their parents), this is a real shock. That's probably because we think having head lice is uncommon or that these offending little creatures only bother people who don't wash often enough. If it's any comfort, head lice were even more common 2,000 to 3,000 years ago. Signs of these tiny insects can be seen on half the combs found in Middle Eastern archeological digs!

Just Scrub 'Em

In ancient times, the Chinese developed the world's first toothbrushes using bristles from the back of a hog. European travelers to the Far East also were concerned about tooth decay. They tried Chinese toothbrushes but found hog bristles too stiff. They changed the design to use softer horsehair or badgers' bristles. French dentists thought even these were not effective in preventing cavities, so they recommended using sea sponges for tooth and gum care.

Don't Forget To Wash Behind Your Ears!

When you scrub your face with soap or take a hot bath, you think you're getting rid of lots of dirt and bacteria. But you're only able to wash off some of that stuff. After you dry yourself off, you're still covered with all sorts of microscopic creatures who make their permanent home on your body. Dozens of eight-legged bacteria live in your eyelashes! They're much too small to see, since a line of 500 stretched end-to-end would be less than an inch in length. Lucky for you — if your parents saw them, they'd probably make you go back and wash all over again!

I Smell Something

Men and women like to wear after-shave lotion or perfume, but you ought to think twice before splashing the scent behind your ears. For years the perfume industry has used ambergris to make perfume last longer. Ambergris is a substance mixed with whale poop inside the animal's intestines. Black, smelly and soft, ambergris at first doesn't look like something you want to smear on your skin. After it's out of the whale's body it hardens, grows lighter in color, and smells better.

Look Ma, No Cavities!

Today's toothpaste comes in a tube that's fun to squeeze and tastes pretty good. Back in the early 1800s people couldn't buy toothpaste in stores. They had to make "tooth powder" at home. The key ingredients were ground-up, burnt eggshells and crushed fish bones. It didn't look any better than it tasted, as it was probably tinted purple—with dye made from pulverized bugs. Even today, it's best not to look too closely at the recipe for toothpaste, which includes chalk, paint, seaweed, detergent and the chemical, formaldehyde.

You're So Vain!

As men do today, ancient Romans worried about gray hair or going bald. They tried all sorts of cures for baldness. A favorite one was to rub their head with a mixture of berries and bear grease. A popular remedy for getting rid of gray hair was to mix herbs and earthworms together and slap the goopy mess on your hair, leaving it overnight for the best results.

No Sweat

When you play soccer and get all sweaty, you probably think all that sweat makes you stink. Actually, sweat doesn't have much odor of its own. It gets that help from the millions of bacteria that live invisibly all over your skin. When your sweat mixes with the bacteria, the result is the rich, ripe smell of B.O.

And Always Brush Before Bedtime!

One man who fell into a Canadian river while fishing a few years ago wished he had followed his mom's instructions. After he scrambled out of the water, he had to pull dozens of blood-sucking leeches off his body. Exhausted and grossed out, he went home and took a hot bath. He slipped into his pajamas and went right to bed, hoping he wouldn't dream about those repulsive leeches. The next morning he awoke refreshed, ready for a new day — until he brushed his teeth. He found one last leech—stuck to the roof of his mouth.

You Have A Truly Unforgettable Air

An old French recipe for a cologne suggested mixing the following ingredients: talcum powder, almond oil and a dead raven that had been fed exclusively on hard-boiled eggs. The resulting scent was supposed to be irresistible.

Has This Morning's Paper Come Yet?

Until the late 1800s in the United States, people relied on any odd scraps of paper that were handy for toilet paper. In 1857, inventor Joseph Gayetty tried to sell specially made toilet tissue but failed. Most people thought brand-new toilet paper was a silly waste of money. They continued to use old newspapers and pages from catalogs.

UNDOMESTICATED ANIMALS

What A Mess...

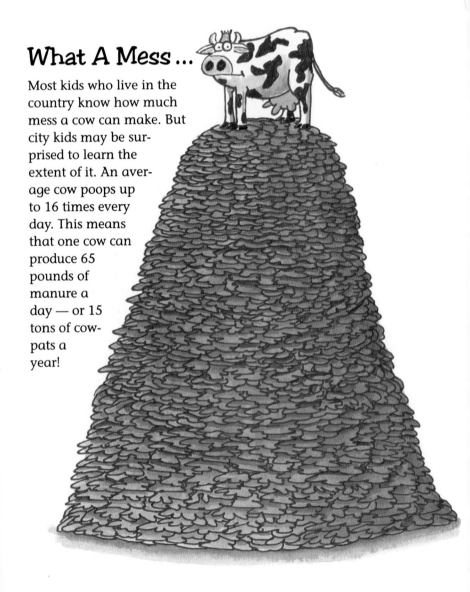

Most kids who live in the country know how much mess a cow can make. But city kids may be surprised to learn the extent of it. An average cow poops up to 16 times every day. This means that one cow can produce 65 pounds of manure a day — or 15 tons of cowpats a year!

I'll Take An Insect Shake With Burger And Fries . . .

Chewing helps make our food taste better. By using our teeth to crush food into little bits, we grind the good taste out of the food onto our tongues. Spiders don't have teeth. They have a much simpler way of eating the insects they capture. A spider dissolves its victim's body with a saliva-like substance and turns the victim's insides into liquid. Using small tubes in its mouth, the spider then sucks up the victim's body — just like we drink with straws.

The Best Defense Is A Good Barf

Have you ever seen a sea cucumber? Worse yet, have you ever touched one? Shaped like the vegetables they're named after, sea cucumbers are slimy and squishy to the touch. If attacked, the sea cucumber reacts violently. It barfs up its guts, vomiting them all over its enemy! Then the sea cucumber grows a new set of internal organs so it can throw up on its next unsuspecting attacker.

Open Wide

A rat's incisor teeth can grow six inches during its three years of life. It's only because the uppers grind against the lowers that the rat's teeth don't grow right out of his mouth. But if it loses one of his upper incisors, the one right below it grows so much that in a few weeks, the rat won't be able to close its mouth. If the rat doesn't starve first, the unharnessed tooth begins to curve back and eventually kills it by piercing its brain.

Bloody Good Shot!

The horned toad — which is really a lizard and not a toad — has a remarkably effective defense mechanism. When annoyed or otherwise attacked, the horned toad squirts a stream of blood from his eyes. He is so accurate, he can hit a tormentor with this bloody "weapon" from three feet away!

Honey, You're So Cute When You're Mad . . .

Not many animals look as ugly or seem as unexcitable as a hippopotamus. When hippos do get upset, they get even uglier. An angry hippo's skin sweats out a red, slimy, mucus-like substance that makes it look as if it's covered in blood.

Hooked On You

Worms are usually thought of as wiggly creatures that we stick on fishing hooks. Unfortunately, some worms actually live on the human body — like the hookworm. It gets under your skin — usually through the soles of your feet, and travels through your liver and intestines. There, it hooks onto your guts and feasts on its favorite food: blood. The hookworm is probably one reason that shoes were invented.

The Pot Belly Of The Sea

The starfish looks pretty, except at dinner time. Its mouth and stomach are underneath its body. When it finds some tasty mollusk or crab to eat, the starfish cracks the shell of its prey. The starfish's stomach then comes oozing out of a hole in its middle. Covering its meal with this soft stomach, the starfish gradually digests its food. After dinner, the starfish's stomach slides back into its body until another mealtime rolls around.

They'll Drive You Buggy

Cockroaches breed very quickly and carry lots of diseases. A single female cockroach can produce about 30,000 offspring in just one year. These bugs can spread polio, hepatitis, and typhoid. Cockroaches aren't very fussy about what they eat, either. They've even been known to chew on sleeping adults' fingernails or on babies' eyelashes.

Haven't I Tasted This Before?

You've heard about cows chewing their cuds. Have you ever wondered what a cud is? After filling up on grass, the cow takes a break, lies down, and vomits the partly digested food from one of its four stomachs back into its mouth. Delighted with this little feast, the cow snuggles back down and proceeds to chew — actually, re-chew — its cud.

So Long, It's Been Good To Know You

Parasites live on the bodies of other living things. One bug — the ichneumon fly — is really lazy. The mamma fly lays her eggs inside the skin of other animals. This may seem like a great idea to mamma because she doesn't need to worry about feeding her babies. When they hatch, they can simply munch on the poor creature carrying them around and slowly eat the animal alive.

B-arf! B-arf!

A mother wolf cares so much about her kids that she gives them her own food — after she has eaten it. Until her pups join the hunt, a mother wolf gobbles up whatever the pack has killed. She then returns to the den where her pups are waiting and barfs up the partly digested meat. The pups lap it right up, fighting to see who gets the biggest, juiciest pieces.

Can The Cat Sleep With Me Tonight?

Over 50,000 people each year suffer from rat bites. Rats are known to attack babies asleep in their cribs and older peo-ple who are sick in bed. Sometimes rats have chewed off fingers and toes of their victims!

A Free Lunch With Every Free Ride

Imagine a slithering vacuum cleaner hose sucking on your stomach for the next two months. That's what it's like when a fish becomes host to the parasitic lamprey. The eel-like creature, which can grow to 3 feet long, attaches to a lake trout's side by sucking with its jawless, circular mouth. Inside its mouth are rasps that bore a hole in the fish's flesh, so the lamprey can suck its host's blood. The free lunch and the free ride can last for a few months without the lamprey ever having to swim a stroke.

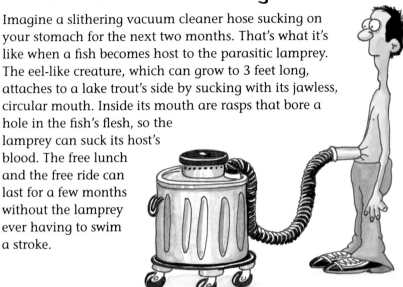

A Roll In The Clover – After Cow Processing

Have you ever seen a dog rolling in cow poop? Kind of peculiar, don't you think? The domestic dog comes from a long line of predators. It's part of his instinct to hunt, and he doesn't want his prey — squirrels or rabbits — to know that he's sneaking up on them. Since most animals have a keen sense of smell, the dog masks the way he smells with a little roll in the manure pile. Quite the trick, wouldn't you say?

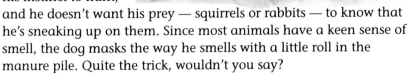

MIND YOUR MANNERS

This Is A Fine Romance . . .

In Medieval Europe, everyone — even noble ladies — had fleas.
Bathing was infrequent, so people were pretty dirty and often infest-
ed with all sorts of creepy crawlies. It was a mark of good breeding
and an honor, for a lady's boyfriend to help her hunt for — and kill
— fleas that hopped around on her skin, hair and clothes!

Let Me Lend You My Hanky

Etiquette books written during the Middle Ages tell us a lot about polite behavior in the 1500s. One author

warns against blowing your nose on the tablecloth, on the sleeve of your jacket, or into your fingers. People were told that it was bad manners to spit or cough into a serving dish full of food. Another no-no was picking at their teeth with the point of a knife.

Care For A Toothpick?

In France, as late as the 1880s, people gargled and rinsed their mouths after eating — right at the dinner table! Water bowls and small saucers were put out for this purpose. Everyone made sure that they rinsed well, sometimes sticking a finger into their mouths to be sure to get any small pieces of food still stick-ing to their teeth!

I'll Have Some More Of That

The ancient Romans were known for feasting and purging — a polite way of saying they stuck their fingers down their throats so they'd blow lunch. Then they could eat some more. The Adelie penguin is a lot like those ancient Romans. It loves the taste and smell of fish so much that it barfs whenever possible just so it can eat again.

Did You Wash Your Hands?

Parents today object when they see kids picking their noses — it's considered very impolite. During the Middle Ages, putting your fingers in your nose to clean it out was O.K. However, one book of manners written in the 1500s advised: "If, in clearing the nose with two fingers, some matter falls on the ground, it should be immediately ground under foot."

Spitting Or Non-Spitting Section?

Nobody likes to see others spit, especially tobacco juice. In early America, special chairs were used by people who chewed or smoked tobacco and wished to spit politely. The chairs had small drawers in them that could be spit into discreetly, then emptied later once they were filled with brown, sticky phlegm.

Haven't You Finished Chewing My Fingernails Yet?

In the 1700s, natives of an island off the coast of east Africa had a custom of saving their fingernails — for their servants to eat. These servants were special and had only one job: to eat their master's broken-off fingernails, or to drink any blood he lost from wounds. If his servant wasn't around when these things happened, the master would save his blood or nails so the servant could drink or eat them later.

White Meat, Or Dark?

In Medieval England, boys training to be knights took carving lessons. This skill was important. Meat was the main dish at banquets and had to be sliced and served carefully and with proper flourish. Carving class included lessons on: scooping brains from a calf's skull, gouging out its cooked eyes with a knife-point, and slicing rabbits' ears off at the roots.

Waiter, There's Hair In My Soup

In Japan, members of a group known as the Ainus are well known for having a full growth of facial hair. At mealtime, these men use small wooden tools — specially designed for lifting beards and mustaches — to keep hair out of their food.

Look Out Below

In colonial times, there were no indoor toilets. Each morning "slop" jars were emptied right onto the street. Because they didn't want to bother walking downstairs, lazy chambermaids sometimes poured the smelly contents of these jars from second-floor windows. If you were walking by when they unloaded the slop jars, you sure wished you were carrying an umbrella.

You Call This Love?

Have you ever wished you could make someone you loved love you back? Long ago, people believed a witch or "wise" woman could create a magic potion that you could use to make someone fall in love with you. One Hungarian love charm designed to do just that sounds more like a hate potion. It was made from a frog's skeleton, bat's blood and dried flies. They were mixed into pellets and fed to the person on whom the magic spell would be cast!

Gross
Odds & Ends

Can You Ship This Package Overnight?

During the Crusades, bodies of dead knights were cut up into pieces and boiled so that all the skin would fall off. This made it a lot easier to ship the bones home to the crusaders' families for proper burial.

Muscle-Building Exercises

When you feel really sick, it's cheering to know that throwing up is sort of an exercise class for your stomach. By twisting and turning, the muscles move the food up and out — and you end up barfing. So think of vomiting as a way of getting an "inside" workout. Now don't you feel better?

Sleep Tight, Don't Let The Bedbugs Bite

Few people like to think about it, but they probably have bedbugs in their house. In the mid-1930s, scientists found that nearly 4 million people in London itched and scratched from bedbug bites. There was little that could be done to control the pests, although one popular remedy was to coat the legs of your bed with petroleum jelly to prevent bedbugs from crawling up and joining you under the covers!

Up In The Sky – It's A Bird, It's A Plane, It's A . . . !

Did you ever wonder how they empty those toilets in airplanes? Well, sometimes they apparently just flush them right out into the friendly skies. A family in Pennsylvania was disturbed once while watching television when a large chunk of brownish ice plunged through their living room ceiling. It took a while to figure out that it was a block of frozen contents from an airplane toilet's holding tank.